1,2,3 suddenly in BRAZIL

The Ribbons of Bonfim

Cristina Falcón Maldonado

Illustrations: Marta Fàbrega

BARRON'S

On Martin's eighth birthday, his grandfather gave him a tiny package and said, "I've been an explorer all my life, and now it's your turn to see the world. Here is the key to my secret storeroom where you'll find everything you'll need."

In the secret storeroom, Martin found maps and equipment as well as his grandfather's travel album and a strange necklace which came with these instructions:

ATTACH STOREROOM KEY TO NECKLACE. PUT NECKLACE ON.

CLOSE EYES. NAME DESIRED DESTINATION OUT LOUD.

"Amazing! I can travel anywhere!" Martin said. So that very day, he went to China. He explored the country and brought back a small pet dragon named See-me. "What an adventure!" he thought. "Now where in the world should I go next?"

Next morning Martin heard very strange noises coming from the backyard. Accompanied by his cat and See-me, Martin walked toward his favorite tree and was amazed to see a strange, blue bird perched on a tree branch. "That looks like a South American parrot called a macaw," he thought, "but I didn't know there were blue ones. And what is it doing here?" Martin hurried back to his bedroom. "It's time to check out my grandfather's travel album."

"Look at this, See-me," Martin said, pointing to a photo of the same kind of bird. "My grandfather took this picture when he was in Brazil. He wrote that it's a protected species called the hyacinth macaw."

Martin stared at the real bird that was now perched on his desk.

"Brazil!" he shouted. "Our next adventure! We'll return the macaw to its home and explore the country." He found a photo in the album of a woman with long dark hair and a man with a gray beard and glasses. "I bet these people can help us. Here's what my grandfather wrote about them. 'Joanna and Vinicius—my guides in Brazil and the best friends anyone could have.'"

Thrilled to be going on an adventure, See-me and the macaw flew around in circles while Martin quickly put everything they would need into his backpack. He slipped on the magic necklace, held the macaw and See-me in his arms, closed his eyes, and said . . . "BRAZIL!"

Then one, two, three, suddenly . . .

6-7

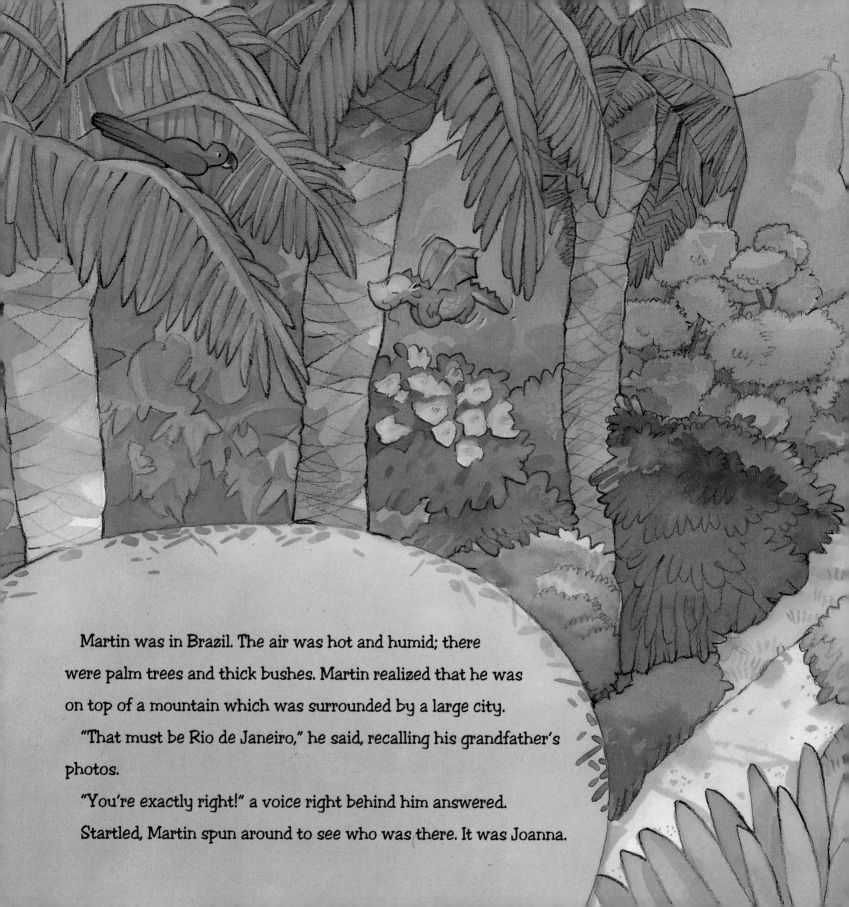

Martin was in Brazil. The air was hot and humid; there were palm trees and thick bushes. Martin realized that he was on top of a mountain which was surrounded by a large city.

"That must be Rio de Janeiro," he said, recalling his grandfather's photos.

"You're exactly right!" a voice right behind him answered.

Startled, Martin spun around to see who was there. It was Joanna.

"Welcome to Brazil!" she said. "My father, Vinicius, and my daughter, Ofelia, can't wait to meet you. And I see you've brought some friends."

"Yes," Martin said, "See-me, my pet dragon, and a macaw that appeared in my backyard at home."

"We sent the macaw to find you," Joanna explained. "Her name is Hyacinth.

"Come, let's walk down the mountain, to see the city and the beach!"

8–9

Vinicius and Ofelia were waiting for them on the city's famous Copacabana Beach. It was crowded with visitors from all over the world. A street lined with elegant hotels, restaurants, and apartment buildings ran alongside the beach.

As soon as Ofelia and Vinicius had welcomed Martin, Ofelia asked, "What should we do first—play soccer, build a sandcastle, or go for a swim?"

"Go for a swim!" Martin said, pulling off his shoes. "I'll race you to the water!"

After the swim, Vinicius told Martin about Rio de Janeiro. "It's the second largest city in Brazil, and it's known for its awesome beaches and carnival celebrations. But..." Joanna pointed to several steep hillsides covered with little shacks, "not everyone here has an easy life. Those are the *favelas*, the neighborhoods where very poor people live."

Martin looked at the tiny houses and felt a bit sad.

10-11

After the beach, Martin and his friends took an electric train to the top of Corcovado Mountain to visit the Tijuca Forest.

"This is fantastic!" Martin said. "A rain forest on a mountaintop in the middle of Rio de Janeiro!"

"It's the largest urban forest in the world," Joanna explained. "But even more remarkable, it was planted by hand after the original rain forest had been destroyed."

Martin and Ofelia decided to climb more than two hundred steps to get to the observation deck at the foot of a gigantic statue called Christ the Redeemer.

"This statue is one of the New Seven Wonders of the World," Ofelia said.

Martin didn't answer; he wasn't even looking at the statue.

"Come back here! Come back!" he shouted, waving his arms and looking up at the sky. Hyacinth had flown away, carrying Martin's backpack in her beak. See-me was chasing after her.

Martin was upset. "The magic necklace was in my backpack," he said. "How will I get home without it? How will I travel to new places?"

"Hyacinth is a mischief-maker," Joanna said. "She wants to show you Brazil, and so she's making us follow her. But I promise you'll get all your things back."

"Right now you need to stop worrying," Vinicius said. "So let's do something special. Would you like to go to Maracana Stadium?"

"Yes!" Martin said. "I read it's one of the world's greatest soccer stadiums."

As they took their seats in the stadium, Martin said, "I can't believe I'm going to see Flamengo, Rio de Janeiro's team, play Santos, the team of Brazil's great soccer champion, Pele. Who should I root for?"

"For Flamengo!" Ofelia said. "It's our team." She gave Martin a red and black banner to wave. "You should know that Pele scored his one thousandth goal right here."

14–15

The next day, Martin and his friends traveled to Bahia, the largest city in northeast Brazil.

"This is a busy port," Joanna said, "but Bahia is really known for historic architecture and Afro-Brazilian culture. You'll find music and dancing everywhere." As they walked along the beach, Martin snapped his fingers to catchy music coming from everywhere.

Then he noticed a group of young people doing wild acrobatics. "That's *capoeira*," Ofelia said. "A martial art that started in Brazil centuries ago."

Martin watched the spectacular feats—back flips, cartwheels, and the highest kicks he'd ever seen. One boy began every movement from a handstand position.

"That must take years of practice," Martin said, "but it's worth it!"

16-17

The next stop was Chapada Diamantina Park, almost 250 miles west of Bahia.

"Diamonds were once mined here," Vinicius said. "But now the park is famous for its cliffs and gorges, crystal-clear lakes, large caves, and orchids."

"And the cave we're going to see is the most magical of all," Ofelia said. "It's called the *Gruta Azul* or Blue Grotto."

Martin was amazed. "What makes everything in here so blue?" he asked, as he stared into the deep blue water and blue reflections on the walls.

"It's the sunlight hitting certain minerals in the water," Ofelia replied.

Martin was silent for a while; then he sighed. "I miss See-me. I wish I knew if he were all right."

"What else do you wish?" Ofelia asked.

Martin answered right away. "My second wish is to get my backpack back. My third is that the necklace won't be damaged."

"You need three *cintas do Bonfim*," Ofelia said, taking three ribbons out of her pocket. She tied them around Martin's wrist. "They will fall off when your three wishes have come true."

"Okay," Martin said. "I'm ready to try anything."

The travelers went next to Recife, another large port on the Atlantic Ocean.

"Recife is called the Venice of Brazil," Joanna said, "because it has more than fifty bridges crossing its many rivers."

After they explored the city and sampled the local cashew nuts, they decided to visit the beach in a town called Porto de Galinhas. Vinicius found a fisherman who would take them in his *jangada*, a handmade wood raft with a sail, an oar, and wood seats.

At Porto de Galinhas, Martin and Ofelia swam in one of the large tidal pools with hundreds of tropical fish swishing around them.

In the meantime, Ofelia went to a small shop to buy postcards. She chose those showing animals from the rain forest, pretty corals, and fish of all colors.

"Take these cards," she said to Martin. "I want you to remember the beautiful places you visited on this trip."

20-21

The next morning, everyone got up early to begin the trip to Lencois Maranhenses National Park. They traveled the last two hours in a dune buggy.

"This looks like another planet," Martin said as they drove past miles of bare white sand dunes and bright blue lagoons.

"The lagoons fill with water during the rainy season," Vinicius said, "so this isn't really a desert even though it looks like one."

At the end of the day, Martin was about to slide down a cable right into the water of the lagoon when Ofelia saw something green swoop towards them.

"Martin, one of your wishes came true!" she shouted. "It's See-me!"

Martin was relieved to know that See-me was safe, but after sunset the dragon flew off again.

"He wants to track Hyacinth and my backpack," Martin said.

22-23

The next stop was the large northern port of Belem.

"This city is the gateway to the great Amazon River," Joanna said, "and a good place to get supplies for our boat trip. We'll be traveling upriver for several days."

Martin and his friends bought hammocks for sleeping on the deck of the boat, a supply of sunscreen, and plenty of insect repellent.

"Isn't it time to eat yet?" Ofelia asked. "I'm starving."

"Let's go to the historic Ver-o-Peso market," Vinicius said. "We can get fresh acai juice made from the berries of the acai palm tree."

"And don't forget the *bolinhos de pirarucú*—fish balls with pepper sauce and slices of lime," Joanna said with a happy grin.

24-25

"There's a *boto*!" Ofelia called out, pointing to the middle of the river. It was their first afternoon on the Amazon. "It's a pink river dolphin. You can see it has a much longer snout than a sea dolphin."

"According to legend," Vinicius said, "they leave the river at night and turn into humans."

Martin nudged Ofelia and whispered, "Do you see what I see on the other shore? A jaguar—the biggest, strongest wild cat in this part of the world! What a fantastic place this is!"

"And we've barely started," Joanna said. "The Amazon is not only the biggest rain forest on Earth, but it has the greatest variety of animal and plant life anywhere. There are probably thousands of living things here that no one has discovered yet."

"Well, I've just discovered something," Vinicius said. "Tonight's dinner. I'm going to fish for piranhas. I can see them swimming around the boat."

26-27

The following day, the boat stopped at a small village of the Wajapi. One of the Wajapi boys spoke several languages. He welcomed the visitors and answered their questions.

"My name is Wai," he said. "My people have been living in the Amazon rain forest since the beginning of Wajapi history."

Martin asked Wai about the geometric designs that the Wajapi painted on their bodies.

"This painting is called *kusiwa*," Wai explained, "and it's our most important tradition. We use dyes made from plants. The patterns tell what we know and what we think, so the designs change over time."

28-29

On the last day of their river journey, Martin and his friends arrived at Manaus, the capital city of the state of Amazonas.

"You can see the 'meeting of the waters' here," Vinicius said. "The dark water of the Negro River and the sand-colored water of the Solimoes River meet, but they don't mix. They flow side by side for more than three miles."

"A two-tone river!" Martin said. "That's pretty cool!"

"We have one more Amazon sight to see," Joanna said. "Lake Janauari Ecological Park. I've arranged a canoe tour."

Martin spotted giant water lilies on one of the lakes. "I read that some of their leaves are seven feet across. That's big enough for—"

"For a girl to stand on!" Ofelia shouted as she hopped onto one of the leaves.

30-31

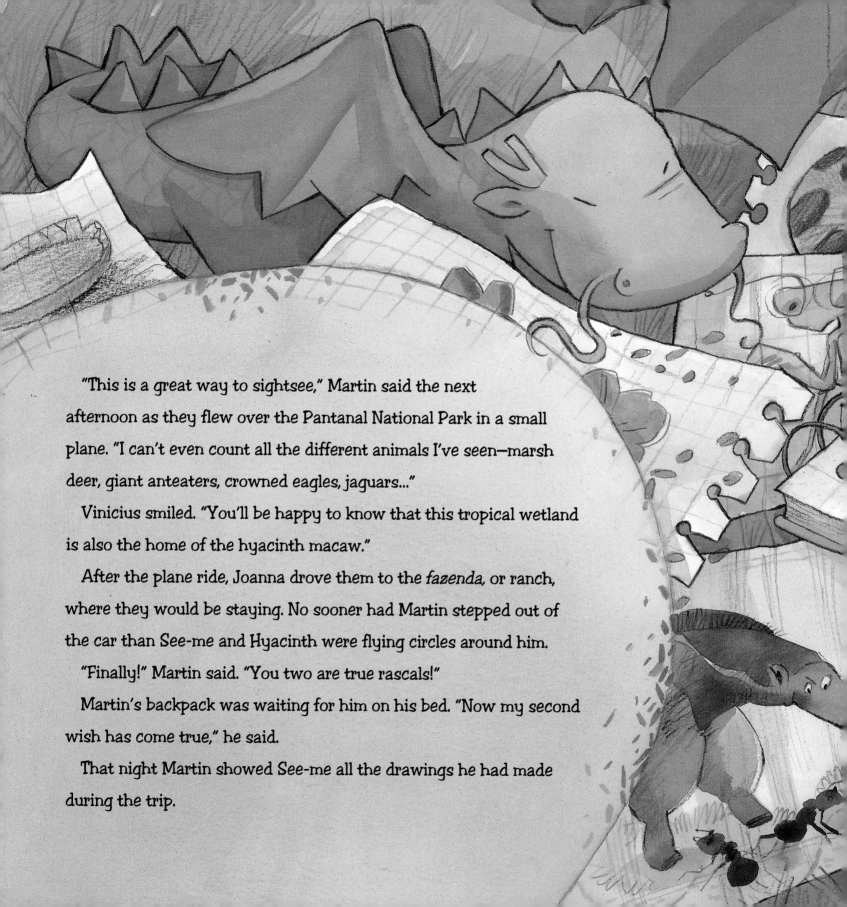

"This is a great way to sightsee," Martin said the next afternoon as they flew over the Pantanal National Park in a small plane. "I can't even count all the different animals I've seen—marsh deer, giant anteaters, crowned eagles, jaguars..."

Vinicius smiled. "You'll be happy to know that this tropical wetland is also the home of the hyacinth macaw."

After the plane ride, Joanna drove them to the *fazenda,* or ranch, where they would be staying. No sooner had Martin stepped out of the car than See-me and Hyacinth were flying circles around him.

"Finally!" Martin said. "You two are true rascals!"

Martin's backpack was waiting for him on his bed. "Now my second wish has come true," he said.

That night Martin showed See-me all the drawings he had made during the trip.

Two days later, Ofelia, Joanna, and Vinicius were ready to return to Rio de Janeiro.

"I'm glad we're saying good-bye here at the Iguazu Falls," Joanna said to Martin. "A more impressive group of waterfalls doesn't exist anywhere."

"There are 275 falls in all," Vinicius said, "but I have a favorite—the Devil's Throat. It's the biggest—2,300 feet wide."

Martin thanked his guides for showing him their country. "My grandfather was right," he said. "You are the best friends anyone could have."

Just before she left, Ofelia whispered in Martin's ear, "The ribbons have fallen off your wrist. Your third wish has come true. The magic necklace hasn't been damaged."

Martin watched the waterfalls until a rainbow appeared in the mist. Then he picked up See-me, slipped on the necklace, and said, "HOME!"

34-35

GLOSSARY

FAVELAS: The Brazilian name for self-built homes, poorly constructed and made from recycled materials. They are found at the edges of large cities. (Page 10)

CAPOEIRA: A martial art brought by slaves from Africa. It is a type of combat combining gymnastics and dance movements. (Page 16)

CINTA DE BONFIM (RIBBON OF BONFIM): Traditional good-luck amulets, used widely in Brazil. The ribbon is tied around the wrist to help make somebody's wish come true. (Page 19)

JANGADA: A traditional sailboat made from logs tied together. It is used by fishermen in the northeastern part of Brazil and also as a recreational vessel. (Page 20)

BOLINHOS DE PIRARUCÚ: Croquettes made from *pirarucú* (enormous freshwater fish of the Amazon region). A typical dish of Belem. (Page 25)

AMAZON RAIN FOREST: An enormous jungle that covers most of Brazil and extends into six other countries. Humid, hot, and thickly forested, it contains a fantastic variety of animals. Its trees and plants provide a significant amount of oxygen for humankind. (Page 27)

FAZENDA: A ranch in the countryside that also has livestock and, in some cases, accommodation for travelers. (Page 32)

First edition for the United States and Canada published in 2011 by Barron's Educational Series, Inc.
© Copyright 2010 by Gemser Publications, S.L.
C/Castell, 38; Teià (08329) Barcelona, Spain (World Rights)
Author: Cristina Falcón Maldonado
Adaptation of English text: Joanne Barkan
Illustrator: Marta Fàbrega

All inquiries should be addressed to:
Barron's Educational Series, Inc.
250 Wireless Boulevard
Hauppauge, NY 11788
www.barronseduc.com

ISBN-13: 978-0-7641-4582-7
ISBN-10: 0-7641-4582-7

Library of Congress Control Number: 2010931203

Date of Manufacture: December 2010
Manufactured by: L. Rex Printing, Tin Wan, Aberdeen, Hong Kong

Printed in China
9 8 7 6 5 4 3 2 1